When the library lights go out,
and the machines stop their purring and clucking
and spinning,
and the books are all tucked in,
the puppets hear the whisper of magic words. . . .
"Good night!"
"Good night!"

When the
Library
Lights
Go Out

Story by MEGAN McDONALD

Illustrations by KATHERINE TILLOTSON

A Richard Jackson Book
Atheneum Books for Young Readers
New York London Toronto Sydney

BUTTERFIELD SCHOOL
1441 LAKE STREET
LIBERTYVILLE IL 60048

GIANTS

Rabbit pokes his head up out of the
puppet box. *Sniff, sniff.* "YOO-HOO! Lion!
Hermit Crab! You can come out now."

"Oink! Oink!" Lion snores just like a pig!
"Time for adventure!" calls Rabbit.
"Oink!!" Lion snores and snores some more.

"I'm not sleepy," says Rabbit. "Maybe Hermit Crab will tell me a get-sleepy story." Rabbit digs down deep into the puppet box. *Yick!* Icky-sticky gum, but no Hermit Crab. Rabbit digs deeper and deeper, way down to the bottomy-bottom. One old sock, two lost library cards, three birthday hats!

Still no Hermit Crab.

Rabbit goes looking for Hermit Crab.
He runs and runs around the room.

He looks high.

Low.

Near.

Far.

He looks in the good-smelling
crayon box. *Scribble, scribble.*
Rabbit draws a picture of himself
wearing cool glasses.

He looks in the ucky-blucky trash can.
Nibble, nibble. Carrot sticks! Half-eaten
baloney sandwiches! Yum!

He looks inside the toy chest. *Dribble,
dribble.* Rabbit shoots hoops—*s w i s h*—
right into the mouth of the trash can.

"Score! I win!" shouts Rabbit.

"Rabbit!" says Lion. "Stop all that noisy-boisy racket! Some of us are trying to sleep."

"You have to wake up, Lion. WAKE UP! Hermit Crab is nowhere. Hermit Crab is gone! G-O-N-E, gone. As in L-O-S-T, lost!"

"*YAWN!* I've been roaring all day. Let me go back to sleep," says Lion.

"What if Hermit Crab got lost in a giant cave? Or stepped on by giant feet? Or EATEN by a hungry, hungry giant?"

"You've been reading too many fairy tales," Lion tells Rabbit.

"We have to look for her," says Rabbit.

"You're right," agrees Lion, rubbing sleep from his eyes. "We have to find our friend."

"What an adventure!" shouts Rabbit. "But we've
never been out in the library after dark."

"I'll bring a flashlight," Lion says.

"I'll bring a picnic," Rabbit adds.

"A picnic?" Lion asks.

"Giants are very hungry fellows," says Rabbit.

THE MAP

Lion shines his flashlight here and there.
Empty chairs, a library bear. In this corner and
that corner. *Checkers. Cobwebs. Carpet squares.*
Up and down a dark row of books, books,
books. "Hey! What's this? A map!" says Lion.
"Or a letter from a giant!" says Rabbit.

Lion turns the map this way and that way.
Upside down. Downside up. Lion shines his
flashlight on the map, squinting at all the
crisscrossy lines and teeny-tiny letters.

"Look! A big green square," says Rabbit.

"A park," says Lion.

"And there's a blue circle," says Rabbit.

"Water," says Lion.

"What's that red line?" asks Rabbit.

"A bridge," says Lion.

"I never knew there was a park and water
and a bridge in the library," says Rabbit.
"What an adventure!"

The two friends follow the map
to the park. "A giant beanstalk!"
says Rabbit, pointing.

The two friends come to the water.
"A giant's bathtub!" says Rabbit.

The two friends start to cross the bridge.
"What if it goes to a giant's castle?" asks Rabbit.
The two friends sit down on the bridge, over
the water, in the park. "Perfect place for a picnic!"
says Rabbit. "*Except* for giants."

"*ROAR!*" says Lion.

"Let's yell for Hermit Crab. YOO-HOO!"
Rabbit calls.

"*YOO-HOO, YOO-HOO, YOO-HOO!*"

"She's here!" Rabbit calls, "HER-MIT CRAB!"

"*HER-MIT CRAB-CRAB-CRAB!*"

"It's just an echo," says Lion.

"Maybe she went to the ocean!"
suggests Rabbit.

"The ocean is far, far away," says Lion.

"How far?" asks Rabbit.

"San Francisco!" says Lion.

"Is it on the map?" asks Rabbit. Lion turns
the map this way and that. That way and this.

"Let me see!" Rabbit says.

"No, me!"

"Me!"

Oops! Lion drops his flashlight!

Rabbit yanks the map away. Lion pulls the map
back-forth-back-forth. Tails flip. Teeth grit.
Ears flop. Feet fly. Lion and Rabbit tug and tug
and tug and . . .

R-r-r-rip! The map rips into one, two, three pieces.

"Uh-oh!" says Rabbit.

"Oh no!" says Lion.

"Where are we?" asks Rabbit.

"Lost," says Lion.

LOST AND FOUND

"I have an idea," Lion says.
"A time-to-go-home idea?" asks Rabbit.

Crumple, rumple.
Crinkle, wrinkle. Lion
folds and folds the
first scrap of map.
A hot-dog fold. A
hamburger fold. An
all-four-corners fold.
"A boat!" says Rabbit.

Crumple, rumple. Lion folds and
folds the second scrap of map.
"A sail!" says Rabbit. *Crinkle,*
wrinkle. Lion folds and folds
the third scrap of map.
"A hat! A hat!
A captain's hat!
For me?"

"No, me," says Lion,
squashing the hat on
top of his bushy mane.
Lion makes a
handsome captain.

"I need a hat too," says Rabbit. Lion and Rabbit squeeze into the boat and sail by the light of the moon over the dapply waves.

"I wish I had my flashlight," says Lion.

"At least there's a full moon," says Rabbit. "Watch out for giants!"

Whoosh, whoosh. "Wait! I think I hear a giant snoring," says Rabbit.

Tick, tock, tick. "A giant's heartbeat!" says Rabbit.

Blink! Blink! "A giant got our flashlight! Faster! Go faster! Look out! A giant"—*Bump! Crash!*—"ROCK!" says Rabbit.

"*ROAR!*" says Lion.

"Shipwreck!" shouts Rabbit.

Lion looks at the crumpled-up boat and the crinkled-up sail. "What do we do now?" asks Lion.

"Pretend we're on a desert island. And we're hungry," says Rabbit. "And we have to have a picnic on this rock."

"I am NOT a ROCK!" says a voice.

"Do you hear what I hear?" asks Lion.

"This rock *talks*!" Rabbit says.

"Hermit Crab?" says Lion.

"HERMIT CRAB!" says Rabbit. "You were not lost in a giant's cave? Stepped on by giant feet? Eaten by a hungry, hungry giant?"

"No," says Hermit Crab. "I wasn't lost. I was right here all the time."

"Why didn't you come home when the lights went out?" asks Lion.

"I hid from Her," says Hermit
Crab. "I wanted to see San Francisco.
Hear the ocean. Whoosh, whoosh.
Stay up till midnight. Tick, tock, tick.
Sleep under the stars. Blink, blink.
Did you know each star has a name?
Jacob star, Kelsey star, Samantha star."

The three friends gaze up at the stars. Then Hermit Crab carries her friends to shore. "I'm glad we found you, Hermit Crab," says Lion.

"What an adventure!" says Rabbit.

"Adventure makes me hungry," says Lion.

"Me too," says Hermit Crab.

"Me three," says Rabbit. "What's an adventure without a picnic?"

"Picnic?" says Hermit Crab. "There's no better place for a picnic than San Francisco. Picnic Capital of the World!"

Lion spreads out a blanket. Hermit Crab sets the tablecloth with READ BETWEEN THE LIONS napkins and pink plastic forks. Rabbit takes out carrot sticks, half-eaten baloney sandwiches, and a bag of squishy, good-for-toasting marshmallows.

"A midnight picnic!" says Lion.

"There's enough food here for a hungry, hungry giant!" says Hermit Crab.

"Exactly," says Rabbit.

The three friends munch and crunch on a picnic
fit for a giant, then read themselves to sleep
under the stars.

For Richard Jackson
—M. M. and K. T.

Atheneum Books for Young Readers
An imprint of Simon & Schuster Children's Publishing Division
1230 Avenue of the Americas
New York, New York 10020
Text copyright © 2005 by Megan McDonald
Illustrations copyright © 2005 by Katherine Tillotson
All rights reserved, including the right of reproduction
in whole or in part in any form.
Book design by Abelardo Martínez
The text for this book is set in Guardi.
The illustrations for this book are rendered in oil on paper.
Manufactured in China
First Edition
2 4 6 8 10 9 7 5 3 1
Library of Congress Cataloging-in-Publication Data
McDonald, Megan.
When the library lights go out / Megan McDonald ; illustrated by
Katherine Tillotson.—1st ed.
p. cm.
"A Richard Jackson Book."
Summary: When the lights go out in the library, the storytime puppets
set out on an adventure to find their missing friend, Hermit Crab.
ISBN 0-689-86170-2 (ISBN-13: 978-0-689-86170-3)
[1. Puppets—Fiction. 2. Libraries—Fiction. 3. Missing persons—Fiction.
4. Adventure and adventurers—Fiction.] I. Tillotson, Katherine, ill. II. Title.
PZ7.M1487Wh 2005
[E]—dc22   2003012801